Rock Farm

Rock Farm

By Catherine Bowman
with Drawings by Tita Bowman

Salt Lake City

First Edition

99 98 97 96 5 4 3 2 1

Copyright © 1996 by Catherine Bowman
Artwork Copyright © 1996 by Tita Bowman

This is a Peregrine Smith Book, published by
Gibbs Smith, Publisher
P.O. Box 667
Layton, Utah 84041

Design by Scott Van Kampen
Edited by Gail Yngve
Artwork by Tita Bowman
Cover art taken from the work of Tita Bowman

Printed and bound in the United States

Library of Congress Cataloging-in-Publication Data

Bowman, Catherine.
    Rock farm / by Catherine Bowman;
    with drawings by Tita Bowman. —1st ed.
        p.   cm.
    ISBN 0-87905-745-9
    I. Title.

PS3552.087555R63   1996
811'.54—dc20   96-1395
                            CIP

For Andy, again

Acknowledgments

Grateful acknowledgment to the following magazines, where some of these poems first appeared: *Bloomsbury Review, Gulf Stream, Mangrove, River Styx,* and *TriQuarterly.*

Deepest thanks to my friends Christine Cassidy, Melissa Fletcher-Stoeltje, and especially Stephanie Strickland and Campbell McGrath, for their suggestions and insights, and to editor Gail Yngve for her vision and for making this book happen. Thanks also to Christopher Merrill. I am grateful to the Kate Frost Tufts Foundation and Claremont College for financial assistance, and to the Texas Institute of Letters and The University of Texas for granting me a stay at the Dobie Paisano Ranch, where many of these poems were written.

With love to my father and brothers and to my grandmothers, Minnie Kathryn Bowman and Natalia Slessinger.

Above all, I want to acknowledge and thank my mother, Tita Bowman, for so graciously contributing her artwork to this collection and for her spirit, laughter, and love.

There's so much war in the world,
evil has so many faces,
the plough so little honor . . .

All manner of life on earth—
men and women, fauna of land and sea,
cattle and colored birds—
run to this fiery madness: love is alike for all.

—Virgil
The Georgics

Contents

Almanac

Scorpion tail waning, lead tree at an arc.
Put the pots on the stove, boil rocks after dark.

Spot polish (on Sunday) the chain-link fences.
Vultures circle, hike up your dresses.

November hath but 30 days.
Bleach fingers stained from the obit page.

Crow poison, thigh cream, the creek is cursed.
Three-seeded mercury ends a thirst.

The weather's quit seeding the day before Lent.
Discount all small metal attachments.

Leo rules the heart, Virgo the intestine.
Starve an answer, feed a question.

Breed, wean, slaughter, and sin.
This patch of shade, our only amen.

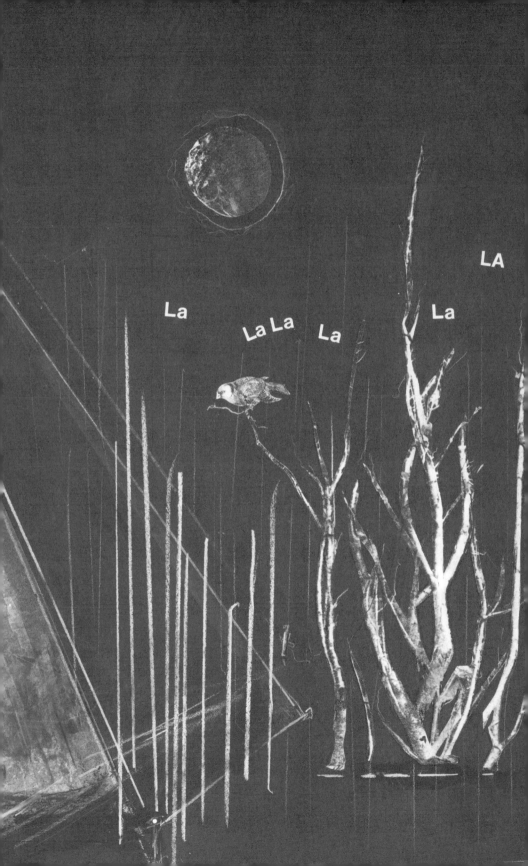

Tent Song

We do not remember what brought us to the woods.
But we were there. You with your funny eyes.

We had thrown away the map and the legends.
We were beyond the open coast. Beyond the cold

place with the warm name. We had left our local
tales at the finish line. It was before the war.

We were married here. The horse we rode was our horse.
The old growth echoed across the ridge. The black clouds

sectioned and resectioned themselves far to the south.
The moon cracked and burst on the pond's surface.

Poplar leaves spooned and spun like silver dollars.
Your fingers smelled like grass and dirt and mineral.

You wrote your name on my stomach. The storm held us.
It was that kind of day. It was that kind of night.

Watermelon Rind Jelly

This poem begins with a cauldron,
then a coffin, then a bed, then a boat,
then a prayer.

Cauldron: Latin for warm bath.
So sit back and relax.
Don't worry,

I don't mean some witchy blast furnace,
or scientific crucible at some trinity site
those nuclear types figure themselves into.

No, I just mean that old pickling pot
my grandmother bought
at the PX on sale.

There she is, sweat over her top
lip, rousing watermelon rinds
with a seismoscopic spoon

to a double-time-sized shellac, thick,
thickest, now thicker than mud-gum,
moan-brine, hush-clove, and fool-July.

Nasty, Grandfather says. Our faces and hands
sticky from feasting on triple-sugar-mountain
helpings and more. Seeds stuck

to our arms and toes and hair. Flies
everywhere. This goes on and on
and on for twelve summers straight.

Grandmother calls her recipe My Famous
Virgin of Guadalupe Pickled Watermelon Rind Jelly.
I don't know why. She's not

a religious woman. All she worships is
money, work, bourbon, and earth,
in that order.

She saves every vinegary dime. She says
if you're going to eat the gift of the fruit,
you had better eat that bitter rind.

Please lower the lights and direct your attention to:

Grandfather laid out in his open casket in full-dress
uniform, a pecan branch in his left hand.

   —A Lime Green coffin, imagine that, says one aunt.
   —More Crème de Menthe, says another.
   —Watermelon Jelly Green, says the third.
   —She did it just to spite him for leaving her
all alone in their big old bed.
   —Imagine that.
   —Excuse me, ladies, the funeral director,
a personal friend, says. I'll have you know
the Colonel's coffin is not Lime, or Mint,
or Melon, but rather what we call
a pale Sea Foam. The deceased
before he passed left a one-word note: *Economical.*
   —That's right, says grandmother
in her matching pale Sea Foam
dress. Besides, she says, they've got him
so cooked in sour juices he doesn't need
some oak or mahogany boat to float
to the place I'm sure that bastard's going.

     Excuse me, ladies, the prayer:

WATERMELON RIND JELLY

PICKLED

O cauldron O coffin O bed O boat
O clove of syrup O mystical rose
Lay me down tonight on the star-filled sky
That is her cloak in the folds of her dress
In that place where her hands pray
Under a spinning world of work
And earth and bourbon and vinegary dimes
For the water is deep the night so wide
Listen as the whippoorwill begins her sad cry
Under a new moon that is our bed and our boat
My honey my darling the sweet sun
On our face and our legs and our neck
The sweat and the salt that we lick off
The skin of this hot July day the words
That come from your mouth and your tongue
The bitterness of the rind
The burning gift of the fruit

In the Garden

She is watching the creatures of paradise.
How the cheetah, in paradise, rises at dawn
hunting the swift gazelle, in paradise,
smothering it with just a paw, then in the cool
morning air, wanting for nothing, eating at leisure
in the shade of paradise. How the hyena's jaw
is so strong that in paradise it can crush
a large bone with one bite to get to the marrow.

The locust, the vulture, the shark, the piranha,
all the innocent creatures of paradise.
How she listens with pleasure to the music
of the lion's satisfied grunts,
its tongue so rough it can mangle
as it licks, in paradise.

Villa Fontana

Villa Fontana, 68 Tacuba, Mexico, D.F. (moderate). Popular restaurant, allegedly once the home of Cortés and his Aztec mistress and translator, La Malinche.

—Let's Go Mexico.

For my dining pleasure, the maître d' cum waiter, costumed
in early colonial, right down to one polished and groomed
gold tooth, an incisor the size of a calf's hoof, a tablet
of questionable carat, jammed right into his boney gum socket,
not by some Jesus dentist but an Archangel numismatist,
suggests I begin with the specialty of the house. He insists
it's delicious. *The Doña and Cortés's favorite*, he persists,
as if he were confessing a secret, as if the oak tables

assembled with bougainvillea and hacienda ensembles were full
flush with reveling tourists and the usual executive clientele,
drowning shell, flesh, and fin with flotillas of Mexican ale.
But in fact the place is empty, except for one harpy-
eyed parrot perched on a helmet who won't stop staring at me,
no doubt directly descended from the great Aztec aviary
that three slaves a day passed on their way to the skull rack
to have their hearts ripped out with a dagger of volcanic

glass, then roasted by a priest with blood-soaked hair, on
a spit brazier. A banana-leaf coffer appears steaming saffron
sour orange odors, in whose innards rests my dinner. *Bon
appétit*, the waiter whispers, pushing in my armchair,
which I learn from a color brochure included with dinner
is an exact replica of the one Cortés gave the emperor
for the sun and the moon. But why is this place so empty?
And could this really be the house of La Malinche?

The waiter asks if I'm traveling alone and if later I
would perhaps meet him for mescal at the Plaza Garibaldi.
He knows a stupendous hideaway to savor the mariachis.
Or better yet, after coffee would I follow him upstairs?
He'll reveal for me the authentic bedchamber Malinche and Cortés shared.
Although I know better, I can't resist, and within minutes
I'm in a room filled with broken chairs, file cabinets,
mildew, and municipal documents. And there in a tilted, dusty mirror

I see the waiter, the light seems to turn him to fire.
And through the flame he says, *I've seen your eyes before.*

N

W  E

S

Methods of Divination

Red sky at night, I should have seen you coming.
But I'm no sailor though my father may have been
as he tossed and he turned us in the rub-a-dub-dub
that rose from his belly, the vapors of mescal,
the cactus incense of Texas. The sky,
a milk-white sail tied to the world's tilted axis.
The world, a deep vessel with a cargo of spirits.
The dead and the living and the animal spirits.
The world always spinning in the same direction.
Creating the whirlpool he disappeared in.
He left me no legacy for how to read the seas.
I watched his two perfect feet slip into the deep
like twin fish escaping a fishnet. Free!

I should have seen
it was you in the currents
of my right and left palms.
Did my heartline spell
out your initials?
Was that you in the vowels
of the cat's sad meows
at midnight in the village,
or as I turned and twisted
through the underground canals
in a boat shaped to form
the Virgin's new moon?
The Virgin's new moon?
An anatomical term.
A fictional bone
in the face or the foot
that would have ached for a week
to announce your arrival.

Last night in the garden I whirled
until dizziness caused me to fall.
The rose brambles all entangled
looked like the entrails of animals,
the sky like a table of dice, not stars,
like stains on a sheet, nocturnal emissions,
like salt, like pearls, like a fury of arrows,
where I should have seen you.
I should have seen you
in the old garden shears
where the old gardener
would have painted
our two matching portraits,
one on each blade,
with each cut
we would kiss,
and the smell of wild grasses
would fill our nostrils.
I should have seen you by fat bees
on flowers like flames
that lit the torches that lit the way.
We would have had babies.
I think seven or three.

My aunt's black rooster picked at the grain.
She was born with a caul on All Saint's Day.
She was buried in red. The mariachi sang.
A man hit a stone with a red-hot ax.
Sap leaked from trees like molten wax.

I should have seen you were coming
by signs, by omens, by marks on earth,
by chance events, by the sky at birth,
by wind, by laughter, by pages in a book,
by freckles on the back, by bumps on the head,
by sounds inaudible, by visions invisible,
by movements of clouds, by movements of mice
behind water-stained cracks in the wall,
by smoke, by birds, by herbs, by crystal.
To say that you had been here and that I missed you.

July in Vermont

I went each day to try to see the fox.
I heard the fox appeared each day at dusk
in the field just beyond the carriage barn.
The field that swam magnetic every night
with a realm of trembling lightning bugs.
The field that dazzled each and every morning
with sixty-some varieties of goldenrod
and the iridescent eyes of large, fat crows.

I wanted to see that fox, I can't say why.
It just kept coming up in conversations,
in dreams: a table, a fox, a ruse, the usual.
Driving down the road we passed Fox Diner,
Emily, out of nowhere, talking about
her neighbor, Stefka, an ancient from Bulgaria,
who called her up one snowy day last winter,
"Hide the baby, lock the doors, I saw
a fox creep through your yard, to steal your daughter."
Then that morning at the grocery store
the counterman's embroidered name read *Fuchs*.
And in the middle of a second-hand book,
I found an old letter, signed simply *Fred XO*,
of course, an anagram, *red fox*. I could go on–

I went each day to try to see the fox.
Then finally after twenty days of waiting
the wind picked up and shifted to the north,
the sky slipped two tones deeper to full orange,
some fumes of something woodsy hit my tongue.
And then the fox arrived, glistening, vulcan,
masked, his golden eyes exploded into gold,
his coat and bushy tail like heated metals.
Then our eyes for one brief second met,
before he dissolved into a pool of trees.
In praise, I picked some pearled white-flowered weeds
and took the path back to my room alone
where I sit now and write this poem about
the miracle of nature revealed to me.

All right, the truth, I never saw the fox.
I went to the field maybe twice at sunset.
Both times for five minutes at the most.
The silence made me nervous, antsy.
I kept thinking about cigarettes and coffee.
Some killer in the woods out to get me.
What everyone else was doing later on.
As for the goldenrods, the thickset crows,
the morning light, I have my doubts, to tell
the truth, I was never up that early.
The part about the fireflies is real.
And I did pick a fine bouquet of weeds.
Besides, the fox, famous for its stealth and cunning,
would never show if I were sitting there looking.

And then that last night in the country
we went out after supper for a walk.
God, I love the clouds in Vermont.
Suddenly you took off across the field running,
the fabled field beyond the carriage barn.
You were, I saw without a doubt, vulpine.

Rock Farm

The cows are all scrawny.
The horse is dead.
Milk and rain are two words
that are not said,
nor have they spilled forth
from his mouth in an age.
In the orchard, leafless and barren,
the needle-eyed chickens
scratch for a living
with their cracked
chicken feet.
The few eggs they beget
are swollen and bug-infested.
Here it's always one hundred degrees.
Here the plough is warped.
The thresher, the seed drill,
the disk harrow, hocked.
The barn, burned down.
The barn cat ugly and always in heat.
The vultures plain fat.
No need for a binder to cut
the stalk and bind the sheaves.
The corn crop is bitter.
No good for whiskey or feed.
The bridle and saddle cussed
out and rusted out. No grazing
sheep to be shorn. No goosery.
No goose-girl. No busy hive. No coop.
There's a hole in every bucket.
The sun makes you pucker
it's so tight and sour.

The moon is black. The stars,
sores. The whole place hurts.
And the sky is useless,
always big and always blue,
a discarded backdrop
from a grade-B western
where one day a strange light
rides into town and the next
the town up and vanishes.
The town that was called New Hope,
then Hope, then No Hope, then
nothing at all.
Where the once-honeyed river
is now a trough of slop
that would be fine for a swinery,
but the pigs are poisoned,
the pig-boy gone.
Now all he has left
is this plot of rocks.
They can't even work as grave marks.
Every night the dogs
dig up his wife (God bless her)
and spread her bones across the yard.
Every morning (God bless him)
he gathers her up
and reburies her.
He stares hard at the patterns
her bones design in the dirt.
He's sure it's some alphabet
from the other side.

And there are so many flies here.
Enough flies, he says,
to build a bridge
all the way to heaven,
if there is a heaven,
eternal harvest
of golden glory wheat,
black moist earth,
melons, sugar corn, rejoicing.
He doesn't trust it. Nope.
He has seen what's come of perfection.
He'll stay here a while longer.
He likes it well enough.
At night alone at the table
he will eat his dinner:
one
     big
         yellow
             dirty
                 onion.
And sometimes the smell of onion
will make him weep.
No, he doesn't trust it.
He has seen in this life
what has come of perfection.

In the Garden Again

1.
The translations are all wrong.
It wasn't just an apple.
Something more French, all sugar and butter,
the licking of fingers, something with heat.
We don't have a word in our language.
The closest we can get is an idea
that would mean all at once
goose-stuffed-with-ocean-cypress-fat-apples-
wind-in-winter-coffee-starlight-afternoon-rain.

As for the serpent or snake,
another mistranslation,
a common mistake.
On closer inspection,
a fancy green garter
of handmade lace.

And the angel's fiery sword,
turning in every direction,
in truth, the rays of the sun,
i.e., the hands of the clock.
They had so little time together.

Later texts consistently omit the *méthode* champagne,
the cinnamon oils, the ocean smell.
Not one apple, but fields of musky apples,
how she spreads her legs,
between his legs,
the really great kissing,
how good it tasted.

Misread and misinterpreted—
there was no storm or thunder,
only a little shame.
What sent them out into the world
was simply the music of crickets
or perhaps a four-part fugue.

What has been lost in modern renderings
is that the word apple at the time
was not so much in the curve
of her hip, or even in the idea
of the curve, but in the heart.
As in: *She gave her heart to him*.
As in, when their eyes opened,
they put two and two together,
two pair of eyes,
and saw each other for a moment
no longer bound, but free,
not knowing, but giving.

2.
Forget the apple.
Since this is paradise
why not something French?
Say, an apple tatin,
with a glass of crisp champagne.
Let's kill a goose, darling,
here in the garden and stuff it
with apples. All I need
is a knife and an apron, and—voilà!—
a buttery goose cassoulet.
Let's get up at dawn, dear,
and work for hours, then
a long nap where we'll dream

about apples or something like that,
it's so strange, so wonderful,
how good it tastes—
like the ocean, here between your legs,
the taste of musky apples,
the tangled roots of cypress,
the wind on water, the stars,
your eyes all over me
like mystics hungry for a vision,
like jeweled flies on horseshit,
like dogs on a deer scent,
your hands on my thighs, thank you, God
for these thighs, the fields, the sky,
the down across your belly,
the apple world veined with ores and metals,
all honeyed and sweet, licking each layer,
10,000 crickets rub legs together
in this world, this paradise
where we are always falling.

Aunt

Twice today I drank the milk.
I tilted my head back,
let it fill up my mouth
before I swallowed.
Some ran down my neck.
I wiped it off
with the back of my hand.

That morning before she left
she gave me my instructions.
I watched her fill a mayonnaise jar
using a special pump just for that purpose.
Her nipples looked like two broken-off twigs.

It was hot that day.
The air was sticky.
The baby in a bundle in its room.
I read some old magazines.
My fingernails looked yellow in the light.
And in the mirror
I could see the stains on my teeth.
There was nothing to do.

So I drank.
Believe me, I saved enough for the baby.
I stared out the window.
Then I went to the bathroom
and noticed one gray pubic hair.
So I plucked it out
and left it on her tiled bathroom floor.
Then I went to the kitchen.
And then I drank again.

No Sorry

Do you have any scissors I could borrow? *No, I'm sorry, I don't.* What about a knife? You got any knives? A good paring knife would do or a simple butcher knife or maybe a cleaver? *No, sorry, all I have is this old bread knife my grandfather used to butter his bread with every morning.* Well then, how about a hand drill or hammer, a bike chain, or some barbed wire? You got any rusty, razor-edged barbed wire? You got a chain saw? *No, sorry I don't.* Well, then, maybe you might have some sticks? *I'm sorry, I don't have any sticks.* How about some stones? *No, I don't have any sticks or stones.* Well how about a stone tied to a stick? *You mean a club?* Yeah, a club. You got a club? *No, sorry, I don't have any clubs.* What about some fighting picks, war axes, military forks, or tomahawks? *No sorry, I don't have any kind of war fork, ax, or tomahawk.* What about a morning star? *A morning star?* Yeah, you know, those spiked ball and chains they sell for riot control. *No, nothing like that. Sorry.* Now I know you said you don't have a knife except for that dull old thing your grandfather used to butter his bread with every morning, and that he passed down to you, but I thought maybe you just might have an Australian dagger with a quartz blade and a wood handle, or a bone dagger, or a Bowie, you know it doesn't hurt to ask? Or perhaps one of those lethal multipurpose stilettos? *No, sorry.* Or maybe you have a simple blow pipe? Or a complex airgun? *No, I don't have a simple blow pipe or a complex airgun.* Well then maybe you have a jungle carbine, a Colt, a revolver, a Ruger, an axis bolt-action repeating rifle with telescopic sight for sniping, a sawed-off shotgun? Or better yet a gas-operated self-loading fully automatic assault weapon? *No, sorry, I don't.* How about a hand grenade? *No.* How about a tank? *No.* Shrapnel? *No.* Napalm? *No.* Napalm 2? *No, sorry I don't.* Then let me ask you this. Do you have any inter-continental ballistic missiles? Or submarine-launched cruise missiles? Or multiple independently targeted reentry missiles? Or terminally guided anti-tank shells or projectiles? Do you have any fission bombs or hydrogen bombs? Let me ask you this. Do you have any thermonuclear warheads? Got any electronic measures or electronic counter-measures or electronic counter-counter-measures? Got any biological weapons or germ warfare, preferably in aerosol form? Got any enhanced tactical neutron lasers emitting massive doses of whole-body gamma radiation? Wait a minute. Got any plutonium? Got any chemical agents, nerve agents, blister agents, you know, like mustard gas, any choking agents or incapacitating agents or toxin agents? *Well, I'm not sure. What do they look like?* Liquid vapor powder colorless gas. Invisible. *I'm not sure. What do they smell like?* They smell like fruit, garlic, fish or soap, new-mown hay, apple blossoms, or like those little green peppers that your grandfather probably would tend to in his garden every morning after he buttered his bread with that old bread knife that he passed down to you.

Santa Blues

Santa jelly and Santa charm and neon
Santa necklaces. St. Nick on St. Nicholas,
and the one-armed Santa waving a hammer
at the Cat Paw shoe shop.
I know he's making eyes at me.
From the valley of the Jolly Ho-Ho-Ho,
a North Pole Polaroid instant Santa. Come on,
let's see that smile, my dad used to say
whenever I had to go to the doctor to get a shot.
He'd say, don't be afraid, just close
your eyes and think about
nightlight salsa Santa baby dolls,
easy-bake paprika and pomegranate
Santa hat snacks, Santa knick-knacks,
Santa bellies and Santas wall to wall.
Those boots were made for
surfing Santas low-riding the red hoods of Barbie
sports cars. And even today when they pull out
the syringe, push in the sanitized,
pull out the sterilized, push in
the blood-drawing aseptic equipment.
Even that Christmas when the sugar-bearded
orthopod took the knife to my knee
in surgery. Nineteen, I had totaled out
four cars in two days time,
a Nova,
a Cadillac,
a Monte Carlo,
a truck,
even then, even now, that's right,
for all minor or major procedures
it's Santa I always try to see. So

I got to where I loved the needle
in Santa Land all bound and drugged and over-tickled.
And the whole world must be in pain
this winter on a snow white examination table,
in this city, in this year of our Lord,
because everywhere I look I see his face.
There's Santa in the subway
selling cranberry incense and imitation Obsession,
Santa cast and plastered at the Bowery mission,
Santa all in black bearing a gift sack
of returnable beer cans,
Black Belt Security Santa decals
at the Autovision Transmission Station.
There's Bruno, the leather Santa
piercing at the unisex shop,
a seaweed Santa at the sushi bar,
a smoking hotpants Santa, a Mott Street
Tinlun Meat Market Santa,
an Aquamotion Santa, a hand-carved
Renaissance wood Santa cuing up
on a drop pocket pool table–
There is *no sanity clause.* Go on
to the Santa Botanica, take your pill
with a Caribbean Santa in grenadine espadrilles.
Because tonight a woman way out
on the plains is loading up her
silver Pathfinder, hoping to sell her wares
at the annual Christmas Crafts Fair.
She's spent her last few dollars
on a six-foot Christmas tree,
and covered it with starfish Santas,
St. Moritz Santas glittering on skis,
full-moon Santas with little glass feet,
cloved merman Santas, berry-stained,
snake Santas with milk-colored fangs, hundreds
of Savior Santas staring from this scotch pine pyramid,
their eyes all shining in the dark.

One morning she sat by the window praying,
and as she prayed, the sky cracked open
and the dove of God flew down and began
to feast on her heart.
Yes, Santa, the world hurts
and the doctor's taking longer and
longer vacations and his medicine is so expensive.
From Santa Monica to Santa Fe to the Saint Lawrence Seaway
there's no room in the hospital
for this couple on a donkey.
Mr. President Santa, Mr. Court Justice Santa,
Professor Emeritus Santa, Very Reverend, Mr. Right
Reverend, Most Reverend Santa, Hold-Me-
in-the-Hollow-of-Thy-Hand Santa, Overawe,
Overrule, Overshadow Santa, the Royal We Santa,
the Editorial We Santa, the Plural of Dignity Santa.
But tonight at least for tonight in this house
or that one everything will be all right
because he's giving her that red crushed-
velvet cat suit with the white fake fur
sleeves and collar that she's always wanted
and the kids are all snug in their beds
and she's giving him what he wants
right there in front of the Christmas tree.
And outside in the silent night
the snow begins to fall.
Three men stand on the corner
and sing up to a distant satellite or star,
I was born by the river in a little tent,
and the world is spinning–spinning–
in the loving arms of Santa Claus.

Clove Orange

The smell of orange, the smell of spice
as we walked through the night
not in an underworld or a heaven

but on this planet, lost, strangers
in a town filled with flowers, mazes,
the smell of orange, the smell of spice.

Lost walking late through the grasses,
through the empty streets of houses.
Not in an underworld or a heaven,

the townspeople gliding in the cool night air
through the three cycles of sleep. Through
the smell of orange and the smell of spice.

Their bodies curled in alphabet shapes on the sheets.
Liquidambars glowed in the western light,
not in an underworld or a heaven.

It was the 95th day of the year according
to our calendar. You kissed me. It was Easter—
the smell of orange, the smell of spice.

The moon waned, Jupiter rose at sunset.
Bright Venus set in the west.
Not in an underworld or a heaven.
Your kiss, the spice, the orange.

I took an orange from the tree.
I brought the orange back home with me.
I pierced the orange with a clove spice.
I put the orange to my face to breathe.

Don't even name a dance after this.
Wipe it from the records.
Throw the stamps away.
Smash the plates.
Erase it, forget it.
Hush.

Methods of Burial

When you see me in a dream
don't think of it as a message.
Although as one of the dead
that's my expected mode of travel.

Don't shave your head
or let your hair grow unruly.
Your hair has always been kind of wild.
I liked that about you.

Don't pierce yourself
or put pebbles in your shoes.
Don't bind your belly with bark
or eat great quantities of meat.

Don't cover the furniture with sheets
or bake sweet funeral cakes.
As for liquor, forget it.
Who said whiskey's good for grief?

Don't burn my things.
I know that's what I requested.
There's a drought this time of year.
Even if on the surface

everything seems under control,
deep down roots can ignite,
whole towns destroyed in an instant.
We have to be careful of our actions.

In a few days when blackbirds and thunder cover the house
don't take this as an omen that I am somehow present.
Even though birds and percussion
are common signs for transition.

Remember last fall when we watched
the same event together–the blackbirds, hundreds,
the thunder, a fire burning in the distance–
remember, it made us happy, didn't it?

Tootsie, the Sun Queen

sugar babies and chiffon fat bees embroidered on a sugared apron Aunt Tootsie's whipping up meringue licking off the dish her buttery fingers untangling the yellow threads of a Pancho Villa marionette a baby blue rosary sweater set with a nurse's kit to match sweetie here's some Kleenex don't forget to wipe from front to back splish splash here comes Kiki all wet burying his face in her yum-yum hula hoop halo Zsa-Zsa oops! egg whites drip drop all over the Easter basket grass apricot toes little x's and o's slipping and sliding over the linoleum floor Hank Williams beer on the rocks five o'clock rodeo dirty dancing darling lover it's a mad mad mad mad world double feature pills at the drive-in everyone get in the playpen all at once clean out

TOOTSiE

the chicken coop and close the back door screen she sings the AC's on parakeets flying free forget about sunnyside up she says its hot enough outside to fry both your father's huevos Tootsie giggles and giggles Mrs. Alton D bookkeeper Yvonne Sun Carnival Queen on the desert the technicolor sky in crinolines behind her the poplars lemon scent baby aspirin pointy bra menthol kitty cats all white leather bibles an avocado tight shift with just a squeeze so sleepy nylon nighties the Jesus and Mary Academy's honeybunch precious angel so sleepy so sleepy all the round and real and imaginary numbers she loves she loves bread and butter and toast and jam and lots and lots and lots of frosted pink lipstick.

From *The El Paso Times*
"World of Women"

The bride wore a gown
of ivory satin.
On the figurine bodice
an appliquéd yoke
of imported lace.
The bouffant skirt extended
into a cathedral train.
The veil caught
to a petal-point crown.

The bridal attendants were in jewel-toned
waltz-length gowns of taffeta.
Their tiny hats matched.

The mother of the bride
chose a bronze sheath
and one gold orchid.
Her hat was of black feathers
with black accessories.

The mother of the groom
wore a peacock blue frock.
Her accessories were white,
her corsage—gardenias.

Fashion Statement

This year's fragrance is a haunting scent,
embodying all the nuance of a war victim's last breath,
the subtle zest of gunchamber grease, a cherry-red sheath,
the bourbon and sweat of a melancholy vet.
A colonial bouquet, unisex, the perfect gift.

We're all so excited by the new evening dresses,
realigned hemlines, inspired by the pinpoint
precision of a search-and-destroy mission,
the patterns explode with the urgent scorched tones
of a sortie-clad sky above a burnt-orange desert.

Other style options include the crack vial vest.
Each and every pastel-capped amulet painstakingly
selected by an army of homeless the designer contracts.
Skilled immigrants acid-boil and hand-stitch each CVV.
Exclusively this spring at Bergdorf's and Saks.

Underwear has never been more risque, more thrilling.
A Seventh Avenue showroom was blown away
as male models in boots and boxers marched
down the runway to a sample of Dr. King
blasting, *Free at last! Free at last!*

Oh the glamour of war!
A new mandate for style arises as designers
in their design rooms capture the graphic
textures that all at once recall an evening burial,
all breeze, all elegance. The energy, the elan

of a high-noon car bomb. The tough vulnerability
of a boy blinded by a bullet. A floral onslaught.
The elongated funeral frock with matching layette.
The ash-enlaced stripped-down silhouette of a burning bride
in nothing but a burning bridal chemisette.

Quite naturally white is the color this season.
The waltz-length white party dress (chemically bruised
and stressed), reminiscent of the bed sheets the bereaved
toss and turn in. The hunting glove in soft kidskin.
The fields of prayer scarves in bone-bleached linen.

Remember, the belt should be worn on the hip
like a 30-bullet magazine. As for skirts:
trussed and clipped. As for the neckline: slit.
Skin: scarred or pierced. *Paradox* defines
couture this season. You know, that dreamy-o-so-

creamy world where one can look at violence from afar
and yet still somehow participate in it.
And don't forget the crown of the collection,
the translucent gown, crystalline, luminescent,
a layering of fabrications, made entirely of tears.

And the River

On this side of the river we kill with garden hoes.
On this side of the river we use automatic pistols.

On this side of the river we kill until nightfall.
On this side of the river we move through the night with the killers so as not to be killed.

On this side of the river investigators develop dossiers on massive suffering.
On this side of the river tribunals form to review crimes against humanity.

On this side of the river we dance before a massacre.
On this side of the river we slaughter first then carry on after.

And the body collectors' colorful hats and scarves!
And the body collectors' colorful scarves and hats!

And the river: gagged & drunk & furious,
with plasma, seed, lung, fear,
and so on, and so forth. Burning
with hair, etc., femora, playing cards,
bird augers, rumor, etc., illusion,
fat, etc., crucifixes. Transporting the dead,
as always, with their cargoes of secrets,
as usual, these fallen constellations,
transubstantiating to silt, to salt,
what will be, will be, on this river,
gorged with wax, money, shovels, etc., surgical tools,
toasters, etc., etc., all the bad luck numbers,
guilty verdicts, verbs, and so on, harps, trumpets,
the blue soaked threads of a gingham dress.

Lament

When the whippoorwill cries.
When the stars shine at dusk.
When the flies swarm on the kitchen screen.
When the house cat breathes in the baby's face.
When every autumn dead crickets, dead spiders,
the horned toad spitting blood.
Blessed are the dead the rain falls on.
Sing of scorpions, of freight trains.
Sing of the cold, cold river,
where the current carried you away
in a cypress tree cradle.
Sing of cornstalks and bedsheets
and drawers full of maps,
of untouched coins and doorknobs
and the supper table.
Sing now like the crazy, black grackles
with their oily, black feathers,
who rise up all at once to fly
in some strange direction
turning the sky dark.
Sing like the little, brown sparrow.
Sing to me now if you can,
through a sky gone dark.

51

Snake Farm, the Opera

12 farmers arrive at the door, each carrying a pitchfork.

We're here to inform you, darling,
this place is literally crawling.
And we do not mean that metaphorically.
You should not be in a place like this alone.

> Beware the tightly wound shadows
> on the juniper savannah.
> Beware the branches, the trees,
> the fork in the road.

Give up all thoughts
of sleep or relaxation.
Do not unfix your vision from the earth
or floor or any riverine design.

> Beware the wavelets of river rain.
> Beware the dregs below.
> Beware the crescent moon sliding over
> the wings of dwarf palmetto.

Stay inside with all the lights on.
Do not let your eyes deceive you.
They are here. They are real.
Who will hold you, dear?

Beware! They are out to cut a way
home right through to your soul.
Beware the lumens in the heavens,
the tears down the face, your warm veins. Beware!

These creatures possess body
heat glands so sensitive they can
in an instant differentiate
between what is dead and what is living.

Hard-Luck Resume

Thirteen persons once sat at my table.
Year before last I heard thunder in winter.
Often I take the last piece of cake
and leave knife and fork crosswise on my plate.
I wear old clothes on Easter Sunday.
My hobbies include sitting sideways on graves.
I put on my left shoe ahead of my right.
I walk in the front door and leave by the back.
I sneeze on request between midnight and noon.
I take off the ring from my best friend's finger.
I married three times, it was always in May.
I stumble in the morning
and when beginning a journey.

1015, the Texas Trophy Onion

Just outside Weslaco
past the Dangerous Curve sign
on the road to Old Progresso
near the Valley-Ho Motel.
You know the one we stayed in
about this time last year.
There's a piece of wood
says Sweet and Yellow For Sale.
Mexico 40¢, Texas 35,
I'm talking about the onion here.
The 1015. The Texas Trophy.
Though big and plain in appearance,
they're sugary and full of water.
Stick one in the fridge overnight,
next day at the pool pull it out
and eat it sliced as if it were a juicy, sour fruit.
Just think, an onion you can sink your teeth into.
And say you're in a quarrel
with a friend or lover,
just grab one from the kitchen counter
and nonchalantly look her in the eye.
Take a bite. End of fight.
We love it when things are not always what they seem.
That's why we're driving to the border.
We'll get a 28# sack and split it equal.
No pecans. No beefsteak tomatoes.
It's the meat of the 1015 we want.
No citrus, no corn, no Cuervo.
¡Arriba! ¡Abajo! ¡Al centro! ¡Al dentro!
Damn, we love those 1015s.
Now the oleander is a poisonous plant.
But not the 1015. Chop them up real fine,
sprinkle them over a pan of enchiladas.
To keep them fresh store them,

no lie, in a pair of panty hose.
Then hang them out on the line.
Your neighbors will think it's a funny sight.
Go on, invite them over
for cheese, saltines, and 1015s.
They'll change their minds.
Maybe it will change their lives.
One more thing, on the long drive
back to San Antonio,
we don't eat the onion.
We'll be tempted.
But we'll wait till we get home.
We'll keep our eyes straight on the road,
through Falfurrias, Mathis, Beeville, and Alice.
We won't look right or left.
Because this onion can make you sleepy.
It's proven to have a sedative effect.

Blessed Be

Blessed are the man and woman who fall
easily to sleep. Who each night slip
into suits of iron and drop seven leagues.
Who never quite finish their prayers.
For them the stars are stitches in velvet
blankets. Their bed a soft cozy stable.
The animals they count are always domestic,
and number just one, two, or three.
Their navels and eyes like goblets filled
only with sleep. Down alpha and beta,
at last to delta, the canyon where rises
a pomegranate tree. A pomegranate tree!
How they feed on her beautiful seeds.
How they sleep such a sweet, sweet sleep.

El Paso

Christmas Eve

She came to me that night like a lover
   but it wasn't a lover, just my old Granny
      dead now some twenty-five years.

I could tell it was Natalia S.
   by her rhinestone slippers
      and her scent of Evening in Paris.

As I turned my head up to the heavens,
   Granny's tears poured over my vision,
      through her saline lens the world

refracted, split into a thousand
   pieces, I was traveling fast,
      back to my bordertown of superstition

and illusion, where all points,
   all surfaces, all angles of every
      broken mirror appear farther

or nearer or equal in distance,
   where on the White Sands Range
      praying families around picnic tables

in an instant become Hercules
   Missiles, for the compass was spinning,
      I was traveling fast, wrapped

in rush-light and tumbleweed static,
   back through the spirit and smoke
      of Black Cat firecrackers, down

and down through hymnologies of fire ants,
   the multitudes in daily lustrations,
      chain-praying under this tent cloth that is

desert that is light that is desert that is El Paso,
   the passage through whiskey burn and memory burn,
      where cars zodiac the windsheets of highway and storm,

fireships scorpioid and chromed,
   dissolving into a carboniferous horizon
      like prison fare for the sun.

Open the gates and let the greyhounds run,
   light the safety matches in the drainage
      ditches where children disappear,

smell the sage and electric tension
   as pages from a lost book spiral
      in a whirlwind blur, the dervish of lost

songs, lost love letters, whirlpooled on
   the river's mirror, reflected in reverse
      alphabet on clouds above.

The stars fall, Christmas yards fill with luminarios,
   beeswax amulets against 77 fevers, God's eyes
      are everywhere, Granny says, in the ashes,

metabolites, rising up from the burnt grasses,
   in the heatwaves ciphering upward
      from the burning cement, the cypress trees,

corpse candles, coronaed, enhaloed,
   the smokestacks, the gem-strewn towers,
      salt pillars rising from the refinery and smelter,

illumined in Orphic code against
   the mountain's oiled parchment, orphreyed
      skein of orphan night where across the dark

I saw the dead spinning and arcing
   through veins of lightning, heat lightning veins,
      all those passed and passing through

to the other side of life. I saw
Natalia, Donald, Pete, Nanny,
Carmen, Ruth, Doris, George,

Pauline, Samuel, Frank T., Valerie,
David, Ben, Sylvia, Yancy,
Daniel, Martha, J.J., little Rose,

some I recognized, some I did not,
speaking to me all at once,
tongues in Pentecost, spirit-driven

voices, solid light, fireballs, speeding
over the high-voltage wires,
gutturals to the cottonwood roots,

sibilants over jackrabbit hair,
cactus splinter aspirations, hammers
on this hammerstone that is El Paso

where I made my first passage with my
eyes and ears and hands and mouth
stuffed and crammed with big light and sky,

where I'll always see the mountain at the edge
of my left eye, the big A for Anne, my beautiful
laughing skinny mother's middle name,

who taught me to pray in El Paso,
where I'm always traveling every minute
of every night and day,

open wide the gates
and let the greyhounds run,
light the safety matches,

the corona of cypress branches,
for God's eyes are everywhere,
my Granny's mineral tears.

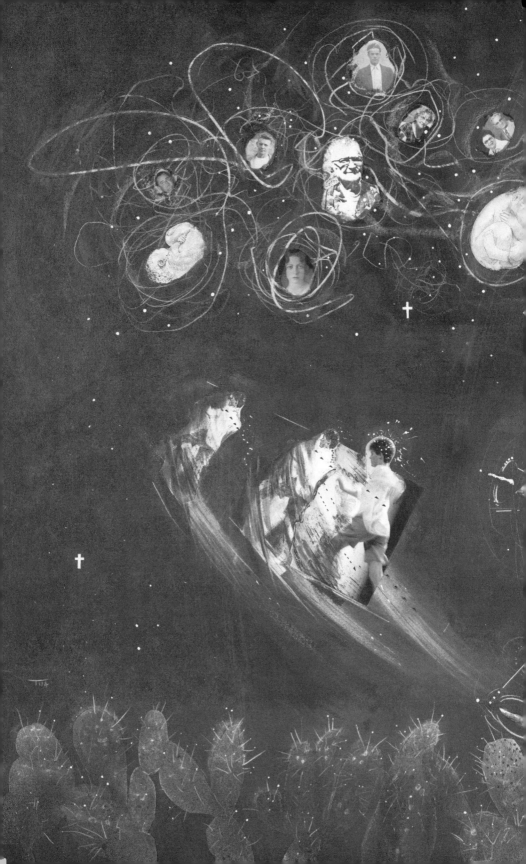

Catherine Bowman was born in El Paso, Texas. Her work has appeared in *The Paris Review, The Kenyon Review, TriQuarterly, River Styx,* and *The Best American Poetry, 1989, 1994, 1995.* Her collection of poems, *1-800-HOT-RIBS,* won the Peregrine Smith Poetry Prize and the Kate Frost Tufts Discovery Award. She currently lives in New York City, where she teaches and hosts a series on poetry for National Public Radio's *All Things Considered.*

Tita Bowman was born in Chihuahua, Mexico, and grew up in El Paso, Texas. After raising three children she earned her BFA in 1992. Her sculptures have won several awards and have been exhibited in museums, juried and invitational shows, and alternative spaces. She lives in Grey Forest, Texas.